The Secret Disclosed

A Legend of St. Edmund's Abbey

Margaretta Greene

with an introduction
by

Francis Young

ST JURMIN
PRESS

First published by Samuel Gross, Bury St Edmunds in 1861

First published 2019
St Jurmin Press
Peterborough, United Kingdom

A catalogue record for this book is available from the British Library

ISBN 978-0-9926404-7-7

For Megan

Contents

List of illustrations

Fig. 6: The Abbot's Palace in 1720 (from John Battely's *Antiquitates S. Edmundi Burgi*)

Fig. 7: Tomb of William Carew in St Mary's church (from Samuel Tymms's *Architectural and Historical Account of the Church of St. Mary, Bury St. Edmunds*)

Introduction

Francis Young

The Secret Disclosed is a short supernatural novella set in fifteenth-century Bury St Edmunds, written and published privately (and anonymously) in 1861 by Margaretta Greene, a member of the family that founded the Greene King brewery (and would later produce the novelist Graham Greene). The book interwove real historical events (around the death of Humphrey, duke of Gloucester in 1447) with fiction. Greene's novella proved influential in generating and perpetuating local folklore of ghosts, and in February 1862 the book even provoked a near riot when people keen to see the ghost of its heroine, Maude Carew, packed into the town's Great Churchyard.

The tale of Maude Carew created by Margaretta Greene has been re-told many times since, while Maude herself has developed into the

Fig. 1: Margaretta Greene's house in the west front today

infamous 'Grey Lady' of Bury St Edmunds. However, Greene's original novella has never been republished until now, and few copies survive of this very scarce work.[1] This edition reproduces the original text of Greene's novella in its entirety.

---

[1] I am aware of only three copies of the book in public collections: at the Ipswich and Bury St Edmunds branches of the Suffolk Record Offices at in Cambridge University Library.

Meanwhile, the introduction outlines the life of the book's author, Margaretta Greene, as well as exploring the historical, archaeological and literary context of a book whose local influence endures to this day.

Margaretta Greene

Margaretta Catherine Greene (1837–89) was born in Bury St Edmunds on 29 May 1837, the eldest daughter of John Greene (1810–67) and his first wife, Margaretta. Her father, John Greene, was a younger son of Benjamin Greene (1780–1860), who founded the brewery that would become Greene King. Margaretta Greene's cousin Edward Greene was MP for Bury St Edmunds between 1865 and 1885, while the novelist Graham Greene was a great-nephew.[2] John Greene served as Mayor of Bury St Edmunds in 1841 and 1852–3, and as a magistrate. John Greene owned a newspaper and was Vice President of the Bury Athenaeum, patronising regular educational lectures.[3] However, John Greene also had an active interest in antiquarianism

---

[2] Wilson, R. G., 'Greene family (*per.* 1801–1920)', *The Oxford Dictionary of National Biography*, online edition, doi.org/10.1093/ref:odnb/50414, accessed 20 August 2019.

[3] Greene, J., 'John Lydgate, Monk of Bury', *Proceedings of the Suffolk Institute of Archaeology and History* 10:1 (1898), pp. 7–17, at p. 17.

and was a member of the first committee of the Suffolk Institute of Archaeology in 1853.[4] In 1898 the Suffolk Institute of Archaeology posthumously published an article by John Greene about the monk-poet John Lydgate. Her father's antiquarian interests were clearly shared by Margaretta Greene, who incorporated much historical detail (albeit much of it inaccurate) into her novella *The Secret Disclosed.*

Some biographical details about Margaretta Greene can be gleaned from an obituary that appeared shortly after her death in 1889, which is pasted as a newspaper cutting into Cambridge University Library's copy of *The Secret Disclosed* (I have been unable to trace the original newspaper in which the obituary appeared):[5]

> We regret to announce the sudden decease, at Bulmer, at the house of the Rev. O. E. Raymond, of a lady for many years an inhabitant of this town, and well known to the people of Bury. Miss Margaretta Katharine Greene was the eldest daughter of the late Mr. John Greene, of the Abbey

[4] Frontmatter, *Proceedings of the Suffolk Institute of Archaeology* 1 (1853).

[5] 'Death and Funeral of Miss Greene', newspaper cutting pasted into Cambridge University Library's copy of Greene's *The Secret Disclosed* (classmark 1861.8.108).

> Ruins, who died in 1867, and niece to Mr. E. Greene, M.P. Born in 1837, she lived in the Abbey Ruins until 1883. She never enjoyed very robust health, and since the death of her sister, in 1881, had suffered much from general feebleness. This was much aggravated by the sad death of her brother, the late Mr. John S. Greene, under medical advice at Clifton, where she had gone to reside. During the past year she had spent many months with her brother-in-law at Bulmer, Rev. Oliver E. Raymond, and at one time it appeared as if she was recovering. But a sudden attack of illness seized her on Saturday, the 9th inst., and though she recovered consciousness, it was only to pass away peacefully on Wednesday morning, in the 52nd year of her age.

The obituary went on to recall some of Margaretta Greene's contributions to Bury St Edmunds:

> Her death will be felt by many of all classes in Bury, who remember her hospitality at the Abbey Ruins, her unfailing generosity to the poor, and her gentle amiable disposition. She was endowed with considerable mental powers, which, however, through failure of eyesight in early life, she could not employ as

> otherwise she might have done. But many of our readers will remember the clever story called *The Secret Disclosed*, which, though only privately printed, was largely circulated, and invested the ancient Abbey Ruins with a romance, which has never since left them.

Greene's funeral took place in St James' church, Bury St Edmunds and she was buried in the town's cemetery.

Data from censuses reveals a thirteen-year-old Margaretta Greene living in 1851 in a house in the Churchyard with her father John (listed as a solicitor and alderman), her mother Margaretta Greene and younger siblings Isabella, Francis, John and Carlton.[6] At the time of the 1861 Census Greene was a guest in the home of the Rev. Oliver Raymond at Middleton, Essex (her brother-in-law),[7] but the family was still living in the Churchyard. John Greene was married to his second wife, Katharine, by whom he had two daughters, Edith (four) and

---

[6] The National Archives, Kew: *Census Returns of England and Wales, 1851*, piece 1792, fol. 12, p. 17 (digitised at ancestry.co.uk, accessed 19 August 2019).

[7] The National Archives, Kew: *Census Returns of England and Wales, 1861*, piece 1129, fol. 57, p. 1 (digitised at ancestry.co.uk, accessed 19 August 2019).

Mary (two).[8] John Greene died in 1867, and in 1871 Margaretta Greene was the head of the household at 1, The Churchyard ('Abbey Ruins') living with five of her sisters and half-sisters: Mary, Frances, Edith, Madeline and Katharine.[9] This is the first reference to 1, The Churchyard as 'The Abbey Ruins', the name given to the house in Margaretta Greene's novella. Finally, in 1881 Margaretta Greene was living with three of her sisters, Isabella, Madeline and Katharine in the same house.[10]

The death of Humphrey, duke of Gloucester

The central event of *The Secret Disclosed* is the death of Humphrey, duke of Gloucester (otherwise known as Humphrey of Lancaster), who was the last surviving brother of Henry V and the uncle of Henry VI. Gloucester served as acting regent in England during his nephew's lengthy minority while the duke of Bedford (who was formally regent) led

---

[8] The National Archives, Kew: *Census Returns of England and Wales, 1861*, piece 1140, fol. 9, p. 12 (digitised at ancestry.co.uk, accessed 19 August 2019).

[9] The National Archives, Kew: *Census Returns of England and Wales, 1871*, piece 1727, fol. 8, p. 12 (digitised at ancestry.co.uk, accessed 19 August 2019).

[10] The National Archives, Kew: *Census Returns of England and Wales, 1881*, piece 1842, fol. 7, p. 8 (digitised at ancestry.co.uk, accessed 19 August 2019).

Fig. 2: Plaque commemorating the death of Humphrey, duke of Gloucester on the ruins of St Saviour's Hospital (1907)

English forces on their campaigns in France. Humphrey was thus king in name for much of the 1420s and '30s, although not without opposition from rivals on the king's council. Since Henry VI was childless at the time, Gloucester was also the heir to the throne. Gloucester became renowned as a patron of learning and the arts, famously founding the oldest part of what is now the Bodleian Library at Oxford (Duke Humfrey's Library). When Henry

VI attained his majority in 1436–7 Gloucester came under increasing attack from political rivals, primarily Henry Beaufort, cardinal bishop of Winchester, and William de la Pole, duke of Suffolk. The trial of Gloucester's wife, Eleanor Cobham, for conspiring to kill the king by necromancy tainted Gloucester by association and the duke was forced to retire from public life.[11]

The proximate cause of Gloucester's downfall was his continuing opposition to peace with France, which the earl of Suffolk was attempting to engineer in 1446–7. Suffolk saw the opportunity to silence Gloucester when Parliament was summoned to assemble at Bury St Edmunds, in Suffolk's political heartland, in February 1447. Although some of the details of what happened in Bury are unclear, Suffolk seems to have feared the worst and stationed at least forty thousand men around Bury – a precaution that suggests he may have feared the conflict with Gloucester might result in civil war.[12] Humphrey himself was accompanied by a retinue of eighty horsemen. On 18 February, eight days after

---

[11] Harriss, G. L., 'Humphrey [Humfrey or Humphrey of Lancaster], duke of Gloucester [*called* Good Duke Humphrey]', *The Oxford Dictionary of National Biography*, online edition, doi.org/10.1093/ref:odnb/14155, accessed 25 August 2019.

[12] Vickers, K. H., *Humphrey, Duke of Gloucester: A Biography* (London: Constable and Co., 1907), p. 291.

the opening of Parliament, Gloucester was met half a mile outside Bury by two men of the king's household who told him to go straight to his lodgings rather than visiting the court, since 'the weather was so cold for travelling'.

Gloucester entered Bury by the South Gate at around eleven o'clock and rode on into the Northgate Ward, where, according to one chronicler, he found himself passing along 'a mean street' on the way to the 'North Spytyll' (St Saviour's Hospital). Stopping a passer-by to ask the name of the lane, the man replied 'Forsoothe, my Lord, hit is called the Dede Lane'.[13] It is possible that the chronicler inserted this story in order to adorn the historical events with a satisfactory omen, since no lane of that name existed in medieval Bury St Edmunds (whose street names of the era are well recorded in rentals and other documents). However, the medieval name of Pump Lane, which links Garland Street to Northgate Street, was *Burremannys Lane* (Burmans Lane);[14] Gloucester could well have passed along this street, and it is conceivable that the chronicler garbled an original story in which Gloucester heard the name of the street as 'bury

---

[13] Vickers (1907), p. 292.

[14] Statham, M., *The Book of Bury St Edmunds*, 2nd edn (Buckingham: Baron Birch, 1996), p. 15.

man's lane' or 'buried man's lane' and interpreted this as an omen of death.

On arrival at St Saviour's Hospital, Gloucester dined, and a delegation arrived consisting of the duke of Buckingham, the marquess of Dorset, the earl of Salisbury, Lord Sudley and Viscount Beaumont, the High Constable. Beaumont formally arrested Gloucester, and two yeomen of the guard and a sergeant separated Gloucester from his retainers. At some point Gloucester fell into a coma until 23 February, when Gloucester regained consciousness to make his confession and receive the last rites. He died at around three o'clock on the afternoon of 23 February. The news of Gloucester's death was proclaimed the next day and his body exposed to view 'so that all might see that no mark of violence was upon him'. The duke's body was then embalmed and taken to Babwell Priory before being transported to St Albans Abbey for burial.[15]

Perhaps because of the political chaos and war that were ultimately unleashed by the factional conflicts following Gloucester's death, the duke became the focus of nostalgic longing for the era of Henry V and was soon given the epithet 'good duke Humphrey'. His death also became the focus for conspiracy theories, albeit not immediately; no

---

[15] Vickers (1907), pp. 293–4.

English chronicler initially claimed Gloucester had been murdered, even those most sympathetic to the duke, claiming instead that Gloucester was struck down by a 'palsy' or died of grief at his downfall. Instead, the impetus for the conspiracy theories came from foreign chroniclers, and was fed by the growing unpopularity of the duke of Suffolk (who became the focus for most of the conspiracy theories).[16]

During Cade's Rebellion in 1450 Gloucester's murder was invoked as one of the rebels' grievances, and popular song named the two yeomen of the guard who 'drowned' Gloucester as Pulford and Hanley. Gloucester's 'murder' was seized upon by Yorkists on the outbreak of the Wars of the Roses; a manifesto issued by the duke of York from Calais denounced 'the pytyous shamefulle and sorrowfulle murther to all Englonde, of that noble werthy and Crystyn prince Hunphrey Duke of Gloucester, the Kynges trew uncle, at Bury'.[17] Later chroniclers almost universally adopted the view that Gloucester was murdered.

The most famous fictional portrayal of Humphrey's death is surely Shakespeare's, in *Henry VI, Part 2*, which features two scenes set in Bury St

---

[16] Vickers (1907), pp. 295–7.
[17] Vickers (1907), pp. 297–8.

Edmunds in 1447 (Act II, Scenes 1 and 2).[18] Indeed, Humphrey's death was referenced in the play's original title: *The First part of the Contention betwixt the two famous Houses of Yorke and Lancaster, with the death of the good Duke Humphrey: And the banishment and death of the Duke of Suffolke, and the Tragicall end of the proud Cardinall of Winchester, vvith the notable Rebellion of Jacke Cade: And the Duke of Yorkes first claime vnto the Crowne.* At the beginning of Act III Parliament is assembled at the abbey and Henry VI remarks that it is unusual for Gloucester to be late; Queen Margaret, the dukes of Suffolk and Buckingham and Cardinal Beaufort attempt to persuade the king that Gloucester is plotting against him. The Cardinal declares 'I will deal with him / That henceforth he shall trouble us no more'. In the subsequent scene two murderers (whose genders are not identified) who have just dispatched Humphrey declare that their orders came from the duke of Suffolk. Suffolk then enters and asks the murderers 'Have you laid fair the bed? Is all things well, / According as I gave directions?', implying a deliberate attempt to conceal the fact that Humphrey was murdered. Queen Margaret laments that she will inevitably be blamed for the duke's death.

---

[18] Shakespeare, W., *The Second Part of King Henry the Sixth* in *Complete Works of William Shakespeare* (London: Harper Collins, 1994), pp. 680–88.

There are hints of the supernatural in Shakespeare's version of Humphrey's death; Warwick declares that he will 'do some service to Duke Humphrey's ghost', and it is reported towards the end of Act III that 'Cardinal Beaufort is at the point of death; / …. Sometimes he talks as if Duke Humphrey's ghost / Were by his side'. Shakespeare implies that Beaufort was on his deathbed in Bury; in reality, Beaufort was in retirement by 1447 and did not attend the Parliament at Bury St Edmunds; he died at his palace of Wolvesey on 11 April 1447.[19] Greene was clearly bold enough to go against Shakespeare's account of Gloucester's death, or at least to fill it out considerably. Shakespeare specifies neither the gender of Gloucester's murderers nor the means by which they killed the duke, although the duke of Suffolk (the chief actor against Gloucester in Shakespeare's play) is entirely absent from Greene's narrative. It seems unlikely that an educated woman like Margaretta Greene would have been unfamiliar with Shakespeare's account, and we must therefore conclude that she had her own reasons to turn away from Shakespeare.

One likely source for Greene's portrayal of Duke Humphrey's death is Francis Sandford's

---

[19] Harriss, G. L., 'Beaufort, Henry [*called* the Cardinal of England]', *Oxford Dictionary of National Biography*, online edition, doi.org/10.1093/ref:odnb/1859, accessed 21 August 2019.

Genealogical History of the Kings of England (1677), since Sandford laid the blame for Gloucester's death squarely at the feet of Queen Margaret, rather than blaming the duke of Suffolk. Sandford also implies that the duke was arrested where Parliament was assembled (which is how Greene tells the story):

> [Humphrey] was by the envy of Margaret of Anjou his Nephews Queen, brought to his end in St Saviours Hospital in St Edmundsbury, An. 1446. where at a Parliament there held, he was arrested of high Treason, by John Beaumont High Constable of England; where certain of the Kings Household were appointed to guard him; and not many dayes after, strangled to death without Tryal … at which time, his Body was shewed to the Lords and Commons, as if he had been taken away by a Palsie or Aposteme.[20]

The idea that Gloucester was made away with is not favoured by many historians today. Alessandra Petrina has concluded that, since no evidence points to murder and Gloucester was not a well man at the time of the Bury Parliament, there is no

---

[20] Sandford, F., *A Genealogical History of the Kings of England* (London, 1677), vol. 4, p. 309.

good reason to suspect he died of anything other than natural causes.[21] The royal council's anxiety to have the body publicly displayed immediately after death could be interpreted as an attempt to divert suspicion, but it is surely simpler to see it as the act of a council anxious that accusations of foul play would be levelled when Gloucester's death was very convenient for key figures at court. Convenience alone, however, is not sufficient grounds to suspect Gloucester's death was unnatural.

The west front of St Edmunds Abbey

The house which Greene called 'The Abbey Ruins' is the northernmost and largest of the four houses built into the ruins of the enormous west front of the abbey church of St Edmund, next to St James's church (now St Edmundsbury Cathedral), although

[21] Petrina, A., *Cultural Politics in Fifteenth-Century England: The Case of Humphrey, Duke of Gloucester* (Leiden: Brill, 2004), pp. 150–1.

Fig. 3: The west front of St Edmunds Abbey in 1804 (from Richard Yates's *History and Antiquities of the Abbey of St Edmund's Bury*)

the house nevertheless lay in the parish of St Mary. The house is central to *The Secret Disclosed*, since it is within it that the narrator (presumably Margaretta Greene herself) discovers the manuscript on which she claims to base the tale of Maude Carew; in the story, the manuscript is hidden in a recess in the wall of a 'secret chamber' by a monk whose cell was located in that part of the west front, and Margaretta Greene heavily implies that the footsteps heard in the house at eleven o'clock every night are those of Maude Carew. The west front subsequently became the focus of unwelcome attention from ghost-seekers hoping to see the spectre of Maude Carew, and Greene reports that the ghosts of Maude Carew and Queen Margaret can be seen walking in the ruins of the abbey church, presumably viewed from the eastern side of the west front which overlooks the ruined nave.

The manuscript in the story is, of course, entirely fictitious – a 'found manuscript' in the tradition of Gothic literature, which relied heavily on such fictions from Horace Walpole's *The Castle of Otranto* (1764) onwards.[22] While it must have been obvious to many readers of *The Secret Disclosed* that the manuscript 'in antiquated English' was nothing more than a literary device, this was clearly not the interpretation adopted by all readers – as subsequent events would reveal. The idea of a monk living in a cell in the west front is extremely implausible – the Benedictine monks of Bury St Edmunds were not hermits or anchorites, and lived together in a monastic dormitory nowhere near the west front of the abbey church.

It is no accident, however, that the remains of a structure as magnificent as the west front gave rise

[22] Anolik, R. B., *Property and Power in English Gothic Literature* (Jefferson, NC: MacFarland and Co., 2016), pp. 129–30.

to romantic imaginings. The west front of the abbey church of St Edmund was, in all likelihood, the largest structure of its kind in England, and perhaps in all Christendom. Although the abbey church had a west end of some sort by 1142, the construction of the west front in its final elaborate form was begun by Samson of Tottington, then the abbey's subsacrist but later abbot, in around 1180; the work was complete by around 1200.[23] So huge was the edifice that it subsumed within it the church of St Denis, built for the townsfolk by Abbot Baldwin in the eleventh century. In addition to serving as a narthex to the church's nave, the west front contained its own vast transepts with attached chapels on two levels, and at the end of each transept was an octagonal structure (one of which, Samson's Tower at the south end of the west front, partially survives). These were unique structures unparalleled anywhere else in Europe, and their exact purpose remains unclear. The whole west front was surmounted by an enormous tower.[24]

---

[23] Hoggett, R., *The Abbey of St Edmund: Heritage Assessment*, unpublished report for the Abbey of St Edmund Heritage Partnership, June 2018, p. 64.

[24] On the west front see McAleer, J. P., 'The West Front of the Abbey Church' in A. Gransden (ed.) *Bury St Edmunds: Medieval Art, Architecture, Archaeology and Economy*, British Archaeological Association Conference Transactions 20 (Leeds: The British Archaeological Association, 1998), pp. 22–33.

Although the great west tower was pulled down (or perhaps fell) after the abbey's dissolution,[25] and the west front was stripped of its stone dressings to reveal the flint core beneath, the west front is nevertheless the best preserved part of the abbey church because it was converted into domestic dwellings not long after the dissolution. The west front even preserves, in its upper level, part of an internal gallery along which the monks walked – and even the marks made by their hobnailed sandals still survive.[26]

It is possible that the west front was 'that house … called The Gate House' referenced in a grant of 14 February 1560–1 of the abbey precincts to John Eyre (since neither the Norman Tower nor the Abbey Gate could reasonably be described as a 'house');[27] alternatively, nothing may have been built into the west front at this time. Eyre was in possession of the abbey for only a few weeks before selling it on to Thomas Badby on 1 March 1560–1,[28] and it was Badby who created a mansion in the west front, probably at the northern end. Badby was the

---

[25] It is also possible that the west tower had still not been entirely rebuilt by 1539, after a fire in 1465 (Hoggett (2018), p. 193).

[26] Hoggett (2018), p. 188.

[27] Yates, R., *An Illustration of the Monastic Antiquities of the Town and Abbey of St Edmund's Bury* (London: J. B. Nichols & Son, 1843), p. 245.

[28] Yates (1843), p. 247.

leader of a Puritan faction in Bury St Edmunds which was hostile to the bishop of Norwich, Edmund Freke, and sought to use Bury's independence from the diocese of Norwich (the town was technically a peculiar of the see of Canterbury after the dissolution) to advance religious reform. Badby was the recipient of a royal visit from Queen Elizabeth in 1578, although it is likely he entertained her in the Abbot's Palace rather than the west front.[29]

In spite of this royal favour Badby gained many powerful enemies, and in the early 1580s Thomas Andrews and the governors of the Bury Grammar School brought a bill of complaint in the Court of Chancery against Badby for misusing the Great Churchyard and the outbuildings of the parish churches of St James and St Mary. Badby was dismissed as a magistrate in 1582 and died the following year,[30] although his widow continued to occupy the buildings of the abbey.[31] It is possible that Badby was responsible for the systematic dumping of earth and rubble in the area between

---

[29] Young, F., *The Abbey of Bury St Edmunds: History, Legacy and Discovery* (Norwich: Lasse Press, 2016), p. 155.

[30] MacCulloch, D., *Suffolk and the Tudors: Politics and Religion in an English County 1500–1600* (Oxford: Clarendon Press, 1986), pp. 201–2.

[31] Yates (1843), pp. 247–8.

Fig. 4: Nave of the abbey church looking west in 1804 (from Richard Yates's *History and Antiquities of the Abbey of St Edmund's Bury*)

the west front and Norman Tower that has resulted in a ground level raised up to three metres above the pre-dissolution level – perhaps in order to mitigate against flooding.[32]

It is unclear when the west front was divided into five houses, but this probably occurred in the seventeenth century.[33] The earliest published

---

[32] Hoggett (2018), p. 249.
[33] Young (2016), p. 164.

illustration of the west front was made by Edward King in 1774, who tried to imagine what the structure might look like without the dwellings inserted.[34] The west front was drawn again by John Kendall in 1787.[35] However, a 1790 engraving of the backs of the houses built into the west front was apparently based on an earlier drawing of 1680, and shows that the house at the north end of the west front (the future residence of the Greene family) was a handsome mansion, perhaps a successor to one built by Badby.[36] This house may have been the most favoured because it was possible to use the surviving northern wall of the chapel of St Denis (whose first floor was the chapel of St Faith) to give any new building additional structural support (although the northern octagon, corresponding to Samson's Tower at the southern end, did not survive). The building that now occupies the site bears strong signs of extensive mid-Victorian restoration, if not wholesale rebuilding. By 1863 Samson's Tower and the adjacent house at the south end of the west front were a Probate Registry and a residence for the registrar.[37]

---

[34] Hoggett (2018), p. 89.
[35] Hoggett (2018), p. 98.
[36] Hoggett (2018), p. 102.
[37] Statham (1996), p. 35.

In 1958 A. R. Dufty and C. A. Ralegh Radford excavated the footings of the dressed stone foundations of the west front, which they found two metres below the current ground level.[38] At various times, renovations within the houses of the west front have created opportunities for archaeological investigation of these 'troglodytic dwellings' within the protean arcading of the vast Romanesque basilica, which are unique in the British Isles. In 1992 the Royal Commission on the Historic Monuments of England conducted a thorough survey of the houses, which showed that rooms in the upper floor of the central house had been annexed to the houses on either side, creating rather fluid boundaries between where one house ended and another began.

In 1865, not long after the publication of *The Secret Disclosed* and Bury's brief 'ghost riot', the archaeologist G. M. Hills gave an unfavorable assessment of the quality of the houses built into the west front and of recent renovations, although he considered the Greenes' renovations more acceptable than those on Samson's Tower:

> The once magnificent work is now not only reduced to a fragment of the roughest part of

[38] Hoggett (2018), p. 132.

> the walls of its base, but is disfigured by dwelling- houses which have been crowded into the church along the whole breadth of the west front, blocking up its arches, and filling them with doors and windows, which, not long since, were all of the meanest character. In the attempt to relieve the venerable fragments from this depth of contemptuous treatment, a mistaken notion had lately led to the production of a series of Norman windows executed in cement in the south octagon tower and front of the adjoining chapel – a perversion of taste which has been avoided in the new stone windows of the house in the northern part [the Greenes' house].[39]

There has been discussion over the years about whether the houses should be removed. On the one hand, their presence conceals the grandeur of the last surviving fragment of what may once have been the largest church in Christendom; on the other hand, the houses in the west front are themselves old and part of the heritage and later development of the abbey ruins complex.[40] In view of current heritage policies, which favour the

---

[39] Hills, G. M., 'The Antiquities of Bury St Edmunds', *Journal of the British Archaeological Association* 21:1 (1865), pp. 32–56, at p. 40.

[40] Hoggett (2018), pp. 221–2.

conservation rather than the reconstruction of historic monuments, it seems highly unlikely that the houses will ever be removed, but there are rich opportunities to excavate the accumulated debris piled at least two metres above the original floor of the west front.[41]

Other settings: St Saviour's Hospital, Babwell Priory and the Abbot's Palace

St Saviour's Hospital was founded by Abbot Samson in 1184, although the 'hospital' was closer to the later idea of an almshouse than to a modern hospital – it was not an institution devoted primarily to health-care.[42] The hospital was originally a large complex of buildings; all that remains of the hospital today, on the east side of Fornham Road, is the west end of the chapel, standing almost to a height of two storeys, and some of the footings of the rest of the chapel, which were uncovered and preserved when a Tesco supermarket acquired the site. A plaque on the surviving entrance to the hospital bears a plaque with the duke of Gloucester's arms accompanied by the words:

---

[41] Hoggett (2018), pp. 249–50.

[42] Milner, J. B., *Six Hospitals and a Chapel: The Story of the Medieval Hospitals of Bury St Edmunds, Suffolk* (Ipswich: Suffolk Institute of Archaeology and History/St Nicholas Hospice, 2013), p. 9.

HUMPHREY PLANTAGENET
DUKE OF GLOUCESTER
SON OF HENRY IV,
BROTHER OF HENRY V,
UNCLE AND GUARDIAN
TO HENRY VI,
LORD PROTECTOR OF THE REALM
DIED WITHIN THIS HOSPITAL OF
ST SAVIOUR'S 23 FEBRUARY 1447

This plaque was erected by Gery Milner Gibson Cullum of Hardwick House in 1907, to coincide with the great pageant of that year (in which Cullum played Cardinal Beaufort) and is one of twelve similar plaques around the town.[43]

---

[43] Milner (2013), pp. 19–20.

Fig. 5: St Saviour's Hospital in 1804 (from Richard Yates's *History and Antiquities of the Abbey of St Edmund's Bury*)

'The Priory', an entirely fictional house of nuns that features in the novella, seems to be located on the site of a genuine religious house: Babwell Priory on Fornham Road (now The Priory Hotel), which was a house of Franciscan friars founded on this site in 1263.[44] There was never a

[44] On Babwell Priory see Cox, J. C., 'Ecclesiastical History' in W. Page (ed.), *The Victoria History of the County of Suffolk: Volume Two* (London: Archibald Constable and Co., 1907), pp. 1–156, at pp. 124–5; Moorman, J. R. H. (ed.), *Medieval Franciscan Houses* (St Bonaventure, NY: St Bonaventure University, 1983), p. 47.

house of religious women in medieval Bury St Edmunds, although Greene was correct that the abbey was instrumental in the founding of a monastery of nuns. This was not in Bury itself, however, but was St George's Priory in Thetford, whose prioress owed obedience to the abbot of St Edmunds.[45] There is no tunnel running between Babwell Priory and St Saviour's Hospital, although the two buildings are not very far from one another; the trope of secret passages, often connected with monastic buildings, is a pervasive one in British folklore and it is not surprising to find it in a historical novella of the Victorian era.[46]

Maude's interview with Queen Margaret is set in the Abbot's Palace, a large range of buildings set on the east side of the abbey's great court, opposite the Abbey Gate. It is by no means implausible that some of the royal court stayed in the Abbot's Palace during the Parliament of 1447, although it seems likely that Henry VI himself (and probably Margaret as well) took over the Prior's House, as he had done in 1433 (since the Prior's House was considered the most pleasantly situated of the abbey's domestic

[45] Cox (1907), pp. 85–6.

[46] Westwood, J., and Simpson, J., *The Lore of the Land: A Guide to England's Legends, from Spring-Heeled Jack to the Witches of Warboys* (London: Penguin, 2005), pp. 336–7.

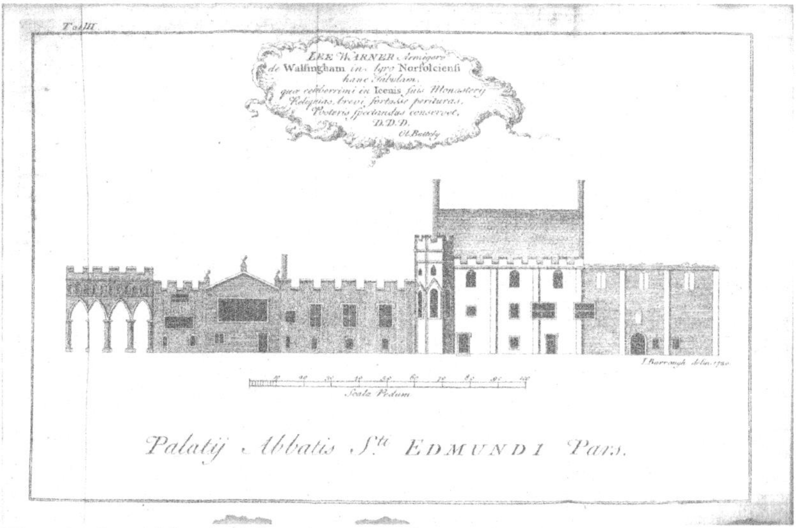

Fig. 6: The Abbot's Palace in 1720 (from John Battely's *Antiquitates S. Edmundi Burgi*)

buildings).[47] Greene may have been inspired to put Margaret in the Abbot's Palace by the name of one area of the surviving ruins – the 'Queen's Chamber', which the location of the Marquess of Bristol's icehouse in the eighteenth and nineteenth centuries.[48] It is unclear to which queen the building's epithet refers, although it may recall the visit of Elizabeth I in 1578.

---

[47] Young (2016), p. 105.
[48] Hoggett (2018), pp. 232–3.

Fig. 7: Tomb of William Carew in St Mary's church (from Samuel Tymms's *Architectural and Historical Account of the Church of St. Mary, Bury St. Edmunds*)

Carews and Drurys

Alan Murdie has suggested that the names of two of the main characters in the story – Carew and Drury – were inspired by tombs in Margaretta Greene's local parish church, St Mary's, and this seems likely.[49] As Greene states in the story, the Carews (who originally took their name from Carew in

[49] Murdie, A., *Haunted Bury St Edmunds* (Stroud: Tempus, 2006), p. 29.

Pembrokeshire) were indeed an influential family in late medieval Bury,[50] albeit not as early as 1447. The family's principal seat in the late Middle Ages was at Antony in Cornwall. The tomb of William Carew (d. 1501) and his wife Margaret (d. 1525) is located on the north side the chancel of St Mary's. William Carew's first wife was Jane Drury, the widow of Sir John Hervey of Thurleigh, Bedfordshire (the ancestor of the Herveys of Ickworth).[51] The tombs of William's son John Carew (d. 1524) and his wife Margaret are located nearby.[52]

The character of Sir Roger Drury, who becomes a monk as Brother Bernard, also bears the name of a genuine Bury family. The Drurys, originally from Thurston, made their fortune from the cloth trade and were one of the town's wealthiest families throughout the fifteenth century and into the sixteenth.[53] No Roger Drury is known to have become a monk, although a William Drury, priest, who made his will in 1471 was probably a member of the gentry family.[54] Greene may have

---

[50] Gottfried, R. S., *Bury St. Edmunds and the Urban Crisis: 1290–1539* (Princeton, NJ: Princeton University Press, 1982), p. 159.

[51] Tymms, S., *An Architectural and Historical Account of the Church of St. Mary, Bury St. Edmunds* (Bury St Edmunds: Jackson and Frost, 1854), pp. 73, 182–3.

[52] Tymms (1854), p. 78.

[53] Gottfried (1982), pp. 161–4.

[54] Gottfried (1982), p. 161.

been inspired by the tomb of Sir Robert Drury of Hawsted (d. 1535–6) and his wife Anne on the south side of the chancel.[55]

The story

Greene's narrative opens with the news of the duke of Gloucester's death being reported to Parliament, assembled at the abbey; a crowd then runs from the abbey to St Saviour's Hospital to inspect the duke's body. The story then jumps to 1860, when Greene says she discovered the 'found manuscript' hidden inside her house in the abbey's west front. What follows is, according to the author, her paraphrase of the 'antiquated English' of the manuscript. The story from the manuscript is narrated in the third person, but from the perspective of Maude Carew. We are told that Maude was formerly a visitor to the court of René of Naples, where she became a close friend of Margaret of Anjou before her marriage to Henry VI (in 1445). Maude therefore stands by the gate of her monastery, located on Fornham Road, in the hope of catching the queen's eye as she goes by.

The queen does indeed recognise Maude, and the following morning sends a messenger to summon her to the Abbot's Palace, where Margaret

[55] Tymms (1854), p. 183.

is staying. On the way Maude passes both a group of horsemen taking Duke Humphrey to be imprisoned at St Saviour's Hospital (a historically inaccurate sequence of events) and a monk whom she recognises as Sir Roger Drury, with whom she was in love before she became a nun. One of the narrative flaws in the story is that the author gives no clear reason why Margaret summons Maude, unless it is just out of curiosity (to discover why Maude became a nun) or in order to reminisce about the past. However, the women's conversation leads to the subject of Sir Roger Drury, and when it becomes clear that Drury is one and the same as the monk known as Brother Bernard, Queen Margaret tells Maude that Drury has been sentenced to death by Gloucester, who suspects Drury/Brother Bernard of necromancy for his ability to influence people just by making eye contact with them. Mesmerism, and especially hypnotism by the gaze, was a popular theme in popular literature of the time.[56]

Maude's reaction shows Margaret how important Brother Bernard is to Maude, and Margaret makes use of this opportunity to lure Maude into killing Gloucester, assuring her that Brother

[56] Höglund, J., 'Mesmerism and Hypnotism' in K. A. Morrison (ed.), *Companion to Victorian Popular Fiction* (Jefferson, NC: MacFarland and Co., 2018), pp. 157–8.

Bernard can only be saved if Gloucester dies. Maude agrees to do the deed and is ushered into a private chamber where she and the queen are joined by Cardinal Beaufort (who was never, as Greene states, Queen Margaret's confessor).

Beaufort is a somewhat shadowy figure in the story; he appears at the very beginning as one of the nobles assembled in Parliament, but Greene chooses to draw a veil over the exact nature of Maud's conversation with Beaufort. This is in contrast to some subsequent re-tellings of the story of Maude Carew in which the cardinal takes a more active role. Beaufort, for reasons Greene does not explain, has an intimate knowledge of the secret passage that runs between Maude's priory and St Saviour's Hospital; however, when Maude flees back into the tunnel after poisoning the duke, Father Bernard redirects her down another tunnel that leads to his cell, presumably located somewhere in the abbey (although Greene does not specify its location). However, given that Father Bernard prophesies that Maude's ghost will be compelled to witness subsequent events in the west front, the implication is surely that the cell in which this conversation happens is located there as well.

Dying as a result of touching the poison, Maude begs Father Bernard to take her back to the priory so she can die in front of the altar. However,

Maude is buried in the abbey church – and this is the reason why her spirit haunts the abbey ruins rather than the priory or St Saviour's Hospital. While *The Secret Disclosed* appears to be, on the surface, a typical Victorian melodrama, the story has some unusual features. It is strange that, given that the death of Duke Humphrey is the central event of the narrative, Greene did not choose to put the ghost of Duke Humphrey at the heart of her story. Instead, Humphrey himself remains a shadowy figure – offstage, like Cardinal Beaufort. Indeed, with the exception of Father Bernard/Sir Roger Drury, the male characters are little more than ciphers who are mentioned but do not make a proper appearance in the narrative. Instead, the narrative is focussed on Maude and Queen Margaret and the relationship between them, as if Greene made a conscious decision to place the female characters at the centre of the story. While Greene's grasp of historical details is questionable, her use of the historical fact of Duke Humphrey's death in Bury St Edmunds to tell a story of female relationships is undeniably creative.

Folklore or 'fakelore'?

Although *The Secret Disclosed* lies at the root of more than one ghost tradition in Bury St Edmunds, there is no good reason to suppose that the story was anything other than a literary artefact. Greene makes no allusion to old traditions of ghosts associated with the west front of the abbey church, merely reporting the experiences of her own family and furnishing a fictional narratives to 'explain' these; the use of the word 'legend' in the book's subtitle is ambiguous. However, Greene presented the story as a narrative of historical events and some people clearly took this literally. In this sense, *The Secret Disclosed* might be considered a specimen of 'fakelore', which the folklorist Richard M. Dorson (who coined the term) defined as 'the presentation of spurious and synthetic writings under the claim that they are genuine folklore'.[57]

On the other hand, and in Greene's defence, there is no evidence that she ever intended to generate a folkloric tradition or pass off the story of Maude Carew as genuine history; this was an interpretation foisted on the story by credulous readers. The difficulty with defining 'fakelore' and distinguishing it from folklore is that what starts as fakelore often ends as 'genuine' folklore, in the sense that folkloric 'genuineness' lies not in the origins of a belief, narrative or practice but in its

57 Quoted in Dundes, A., *Folklore Matters* (Knoxville, TN: University of Tennessee Press, 1989), p. 40.

popular acceptance and organic evolution as part of a tradition. Clearly, there is a rich tradition in contemporary Bury St Edmunds about the Grey Lady, and variants of the story of Maude Carew continue to be told. The fact that Maude Carew was invented by Margaretta Greene is more or less irrelevant from a folkloric perspective. Many traditions of hauntings can be traced back to nineteenth-century works of imaginative fiction that gradually came to be accepted as factual reports – but not necessarily because the original author of the fictional work ever intended this.[58]

So many people were convinced of the veracity of Greene's story when it was published that a large crowd gathered outside her house at eleven o'clock in the evening on 24 February 1862 in the hope of seeing the ghosts of Maude Carew and Queen Margaret, which Greene promised could be seen an hour before midnight on that date. By the time the apparitions were supposed to appear the mood of the crowd was approaching hysteria, and the attempts of some people to claim they could see two figures gliding over the ground led to a brawl, as others denounced them as hoaxers. Some of the crowd began throwing stones, breaking

---

[58] Young, F., *English Catholics and the Supernatural, 1553–1829* (Ashgate: Farnham, 2013), p. 97.

windows in the Greenes' house, and the police were forced to break up the crowd after midnight. A later account claimed that Margaretta Greene's nephew John attempted to stir up interest by wandering the churchyard dressed in a white sheet, but was pelted with sticks and stones.[59]

In the second half of the nineteenth century trying to see ghosts in large mobs was a popular 'urban recreation' and a public nuisance frequently reported in the press. When people in the crowd became bored they often turned to acts of petty vandalism like the breaking of the Greenes' windows.[60] Impersonating ghosts was also popular, albeit dangerous – since it might result in violence or arrest.[61]

The Grey Lady – sometimes identified as Maude Carew and sometimes not – soon took root as the town's best-known ghost. In the 1930s the Grey Lady was associated with the Abbey Gardens, and especially with a Mark IV tank then d-isplayed there. The fact that the houses in the west front fell into dereliction and disrepair in the 1930s and '40s only enhanced their supernatural reputation.[62]

---

59 Murdie (2006), pp. 30–1.

60 Davies, O., *The Haunted: A Social History of Ghosts* (Basingstoke: Palgrave MacMillan, 2007), pp. 90–4.

61 Davies (2007), pp. 168–70.

62 Murdie (2006), pp. 31–3.

Perhaps fittingly, the Grey Lady came to be associated with The Priory on Fornham Road, where *The Bury Free Press* reported that a grey figure had been seen vaulting over the medieval precinct wall in December 1929.[63] People have also reported manifestations of the Grey Lady associated with St Saviour's Hospital and even the Tesco supermarket that partially occupies the site of the hospital.[64]

The basic narrative of *The Secret Disclosed* has been retold many times, with varying degrees of faithfulness to Margaretta Greene's original narrative. Alan Murdie's version of the story, for example, deviates slightly from Greene's; Murdie has Queen Margaret deliberately summon Maude Carew into her presence in order to trick the nun into murdering Humphrey, and has Father Bernard curse Maude before her death (rather than simply prophesying her doom). Furthermore, Murdie's Father Bernard is the monk who, repenting of cursing Maude, hides the account of the whole affair in the secret cavity of the west front.[65] Kirsty Hartsiotis also includes a re-telling of the Maude Carew story in her *Suffolk Folk Tales* (2013).[66]

---

[63] Murdie (2006), p. 39.

[64] Murdie (2006), pp. 36–8.

[65] Murdie (2006), pp. 27–8.

[66] Hartsiotis, K., *Suffolk Folk Tales* (The History Press: Stroud, 2013), pp. 164–70.

Whatever else may be said about Margaretta Greene's *The Secret Disclosed*, its local popularity meant that the novella planted the abbey's west front, and the abbey ruins in general, in the popular imagination. This was something that no amount of antiquarian investigation and publication could ever do. In this respect, *The Secret Disclosed* has a strongly contemporary resonance; just as ordinary people in the nineteenth century engaged with built heritage via stories about alleged supernatural apparitions, so 'paranormal history' and ghost tours are today one of the most popular ways for people to engage with historic buildings. Whether historians like it or not, people continue to link the past with the supernatural; the tracing of ghost stories like *The Secret Disclosed* creates the opportunity to provoke a genuine interest in history where there might otherwise be only curiosity about ghosts.

Editor's note

The original text of *The Secret Disclosed* was divided by asterisks at certain key points (probably to reduce the cost of printing), but I have made the decision in this edition to present the distinct sections as numbered mini-chapters. Apart from this, the only change made to the arrangement of the text as it appears in the original is to adapt the text of conversations to adhere to the modern convention of each character speaking on a new line. I have also silently corrected a small number of inconsequential typographical errors that appear in the original text.

1

It is the year 1447 and the month of February. The Abbey of St. Edmund is at the heighth of its magnificence and glory. In the refectory,[67] a large and splendid chamber, sits King Henry 6th, the refined and gentle ruler of England. By his side is seated his young Queen Margaret, whose masculine mind exercised a powerful influence over her too yielding husband. Near them stands Cardinal Beaufort,[68] in whose haughty bearing and sinister aspect may be read purpose utterly the reverse of all that befits his sacred calling. Around the long table are all the noblest of English barons assembled in parliament. Their office this day is to sit in judgment on one of their own number, Humphrey, Duke of Gloucester, arraigned before them for high treason.

---

[67] The Parliament of 1447 was actually held in the abbey's chapterhouse.

[68] Cardinal Beaufort did not attend the Parliament of 1447.

But instead of the Duke a messenger is announced from St. Saviour's Hospital, where the Duke is imprisoned. He enters pale and trembling, and announces to the dismayed King that the Duke of Gloucester has been found dead in his bed. Exclamations of horror are heard on all sides, and looks of suspicion are directed towards the upper end of the room, where the Queen and Cardinal are standing. Why does the Queen's colour vary from the deepest red to the most ghastly white? and why are her expressions of grief so incoherent? Gloucester was no friend of hers; it cannot be sorrow alone for his untimely end which thus affects her. Still it is natural that a woman should be shocked at such sudden tidings, and grieved for her husband's sake; for he loved the man who has been thus unexpectedly snatched away. The noise of a multitude is heard without – they press into the noble assembly. It is not only grief which they express, but the sound of suspicion is heard breaking out into the words, "*murder* and *revenge*." The crowd of mingled nobles and commons hurries towards St. Saviour's Hospital, near the North-gate of the town. There, extended on his bed, lies the good Duke Humphrey; no marks of violence can be found, no signs of an unnatural death, no evidence upon which suspicion can rest, but nevertheless it is not allayed.

Nothing can be discovered, and the death of Humphrey, Duke of Gloucester, has remained a mystery which no historian has ever been able to solve.

2

Let us turn from 1447 to 1860, and from the Abbey in its glory, to the house built in its ruins. In those 400 years, what a change has passed over all! The nave of the once splendid church of St. Edmund is now a garden, in which the old remains form a most interesting feature. The ancient refectory in which so many historical scenes have been presented, contains at the present time chiefly gooseberry bushes and vegetables. Within the remains of the West front of the church, stands the old rambling house, which is called "The Abbey Ruins." From its situation it might reasonably be supposed to be haunted, and I can assert as facts several strange phenomena connected with it. Every night, at eleven o'clock, a deep, dull sound is heard repeated several times, like a foot heavily stamping on the ground. No cause which might account for it has ever been discovered. But it is a still more remarkable fact that, at times the numerous family, who occupy the house have, when assembled, been startled by the sound of a footstep flitting across the room, and become conscious that something was passing, although nothing whatever could be seen. In the house is a secret chamber, the existence of which has long been known to the inhabitants of the dwelling. We all remember the vague sense of mystery connected with it in our childhood. A few weeks ago, in the course of some necessary repairs this secret room was opened, and we all explored it. One visit I paid to it alone. The carpenter had gone to his dinner, but had left his tools. I felt an irresistible impulse to examine carefully every part of the ruinous walls and dark recesses. My eye was caught by a cavity in the wall, which had been disclosed by the workmen having knocked off a projecting stone. I peeped in, and thinking I saw something which was neither stone nor mortar, I took up the hammer and with some difficulty enlarged the hole and extracted from it a small metal box. My delight and curiosity may be imagined; I hurried away with my treasure to my own room. I feared I might not be able to open it, but it yielded at once to a slight pressure, and contained – not money or jewels as I had hoped – but an old manuscript clearly written and beautifully illuminated. It was in antiquated English, but by slow degrees I read and understood it all.

The writer began by saying, that he was a very aged monk, who had lived many years in the monastery of St. Edmund. He had heard many important secrets, one of which weighed heavily on his mind. It concerned the murder of Humphrey, Duke of Gloucester, who died in St. Saviour's Hospital on the 24th of February, 1447. He had sworn never to reveal it in his life-time, but he could not die without taking some means by which it might be disclosed to posterity. He had therefore written an account of it, enclosed the manuscript in a metal box, and placed it within the walls of a cell, which he occupied at the summit of one of the Western towers of St. Edmund's Church.[69] There it had doubtless remained undisturbed until I accidentally discovered it, and the secret so long concealed it now for the first time disclosed. I relate the story in my own words, as the language of the manuscript is full of obsolete expressions and written in a stiff and antiquated style, which might be unpleasant to my readers.

---

[69] The 'western towers' alluded to here are presumably the octagonal structures at each end of the west front; only fragments of the octagon at the north end of the west front survive.

3

In the middle of the 15th century, there existed near the North-gate of the town of Bury a religious establishment for women.[70] It was called the Priory, and was under the spiritual jurisdiction of the Abbot of Bury. Many ladies of the noblest families in the neighbourhood were then living within its walls bound by the usual monastic vow.

One bright February morning, all were astir in the good town of St. Edmund's Bury, and the unwonted bustle extended even to the quiet cells of the holy sisterhood. For their sovereign lord King Henry and his fair young Queen were coming with great pomp and state to hold a parliament in the ancient Abbey. The procession was to enter by the North-gate; for the noble company had passed the previous night at the large and important town of

---

[70] The priory in the story is entirely fictitious, and a house of religious women never existed in medieval Bury St Edmunds.

Thetford. Crowds of the citizens of Bury in their gayest attire filled the streets, the church bells were ringing, banners and gorgeous tapestry hung from the windows, which were occupied by richly dressed ladies. Near the gate by which the Royal party were to enter, a splendid pageant was prepared according to the custom of that time. Even the nuns were permitted to appear at the gate of their convent to receive the Queen. Among them was one who could not fail to attract attention; for hers was a face irresistibly impressive, not from her youth and beauty alone, or the grace that could not be concealed, but rather from an expression of deep and hopeless melancholy, a look as if life had lost all its charms for her, and from a strange light in her deep blue eyes, which spoke of a mind restless and even unsound. All knew the history of her life; for the noble family of Carew to which she belonged, had long lived in the neighbourhood; but none could guess why she had chosen the cloister for her home. Her father, William Carew, had travelled more than most men of that age, and his daughter Maude had once accompanied him to the Court of René, King of Anjou and Provence,[71] whither he had gone with the embassy to demand the hand of

[71] Margaret of Anjou's father, René, Count of Anjou and Provence (1409–80) claimed the title of King of Naples.

the Princess Margaret for King Henry. Maude and the young Princess had become very intimate, but of all of that had happened during the months she had spent in France, very little could be gathered from the conversation of the nun. She invariably shunned the subject. The cause which might induce a maiden to forsake the world could scarcely be imputed to her; for so far as those around her could judge, she had never known the sorrow of an unrequited attachment. Many noble and wealthy knights had sought her hand, but she coldly refused them all. And yet no one could believe that her vocation was the cloister; religious duties and charitable offices seemed wearisome to her; she had always loved gaiety, excitement and pleasure. No one could divine her reason for quitting the scenes in which she appeared to delight, for the sake of devoting herself to duties which were a burden to her.

On that gay morning, which would give her a glimpse of her former life, and of the friend of her happier days, Maude could not conceal a feeling of unwonted excitement. The Queen had heard nothing of her for at least two years. Would she remember her old friend? would she recognise her in her altered state? Maude thought she would not; for much had happened to both since they last met. Two years upon the throne! two years in the cloister! both were doubtless changed from the merry companions in the revels of King René's court. She watched with anxious looks the approach of the gay procession. The thunder of martial music, and the shouts of the populace greeted the King and Queen; but in the midst of the gorgeous pageant Margaret's eye fell upon the band of nuns assembled at the Convent gate, and the sudden start of surprise told Maude she was recognised.

The next morning a page and two waiting women of the queen's retinue arrived at the Priory with an urgent request that sister Maude might be permitted to accompany them back to the palace, as her Highness desired an interview with her. Such a request had the force of a command, and in spite of the ill-concealed jealousy of the other nuns, the prioress could not refuse her permission. Sister Maude accompanied the Queen's messengers back to the Abbot's palace, where the royal party were lodged. On their way, they encountered such a crowd of horsemen, that Maude, long unused to such stirring scenes, was almost alarmed. The pages reassured her, and told her with an expression of indignation, that these armed cavaliers were taking the good Duke Humphrey, who had just been impeached for high treason, to be confined in St. Saviour's Hospital.[72]

"They may imprison him," added the page, "but he is too strong for them. All men say that his release is certain; a few days' imprisonment is the worst they will have power to inflict on him." They rode on until nearly in view of the Abbey. Walking slowly along, a tall and stately man, in the dark robes of a monk, passed by. We are sometimes struck by something in a stranger which recalls to us, in a way we cannot account for, some one we have known. It was thus with Maude; the first glance at this form brought vividly back to her mind the remembrance of happier days. They were then riding down a hill;[73] Maude's palfrey stumbled; it was only for an instant, but the movement attracted the Monk and he looked up at the party. Maude's face was concealed by the veil, but that of the Monk was clearly shown. He was a very dark, stern looking man, emaciated as if from suffering or hard study; his eyes were black and very piercing.

"It is Father Bernard," murmured the page, "he is a man of whom strange tales are told." A

---

[72] Instead of being arrested when he arrived in Bury, Gloucester made his own way to St Saviour's Hospital and was placed under arrest there not long after his arrival.

[73] Presumably the slope at the southern end of Northgate Street.

feeling of deadly faintness caused the nun to lean forward on her horse, but by a tremendous effort she overcame it and rode on in silence, struggling to efface all appearance of emotion.

The Abbey-gate and the court-yard were crowded with servants and lay brethren of the monastery, and many gazed with surprise at the nun as she passed. Turning to the right she alighted from her horse and was conducted by the attendants to the Queen's apartments. Margaret received her rather with the familiarity of an old friend than with the condescension of a queen. Her first words were an expression of surprise at finding Maude, once the gayest of the gay, in the sombre garb of a nun.

"Were you tired of the world? have you found peace and happiness in the quiet life of a convent?" asked the queen.

"Peace and happiness!" repeated the nun in a bitter, scornful tone, "I have forgotten what those words mean."

"I can well imagine that they are not to be found in a cloister," returned Margaret; "the monotony of such a life must be dreary in the extreme. Excitement is the only enjoyment in my opinion."

"I hope your Highness finds that enjoyment; a queen of seventeen may well think her own lot the happiest of all."

"I might be happy certainly," replied the Queen, 'if my will were not so continually thwarted. Not that my husband is wont to oppose me; so far as he is concerned I am absolute mistress of his kingdom, and that is what I will be in very deed and without a check; I am determined that my enemy, that most hateful, smooth-tongued hypocritical …" she paused, and Maude asked incredulously "Who can be an enemy of your Grace? all are eager only to court the favour of King Henry's powerful Consort."

"It may appear so, but treachery and hatred use the cloak of assiduous attentions," returned the Queen – "however we will not speak of that now – I pray you, if I may use such liberty, tell me why you chose to immure yourself where you own you are so miserable? I had anticipated a different fate for you. What has become of Sir Roger Drury, that dark and stern knight, whom I always feared, but who seemed to possess such a fascination for you?"

Maude had started and turned very pale at the name, but she calmly answered, "Your Grace might reasonably be supposed to know more of lords or knights than I – I who have mingled with no society but the sisterhood for two long years!"

"What a strange man he was!" continued Margaret, "I am certain he possessed some magical powers. Do you remember the strange stories that were told of his fixing men and women with his stern piercing gaze until they became quite unconscious? I can well imagine it, for there was something unearthly in those deep eyes of his … The thought of him puts me in mind of another subject," she went on, "there is a monk of this monastery, one Brother Bernard, who has been accused of sorcery and of dealings with the evil one. What men say of him seems to me much like the tales we have heard of Sir Roger Drury. The monks affirm that he can deprive men of all their senses only by waving his hand, and that no one can restore them but himself. They say too that he knows all that is passing at divers places at the same instant, while he himself stirs not from home. Many and marvellous are the reports concerning him, and so clearly is he shown to be a magician, that the Duke of Gloucester hath given orders that he should be burnt at the stake…"[74]

---

[74] This is historically inaccurate on three levels. The duke of Gloucester had no judicial authority, in and of himself, to condemn anyone for a crime; the practice of magic was a crime punished by the church in the fifteenth century (which could only impose penances); and the penalty for sorcery and witchcraft in England was never burning at the stake.

Maude interrupted the Queen with a faint scream of horror, and starting from her seat, she fiercely exclaimed, "It is false! it cannot be true! Can nothing be done to save him? Oh! how fearful! how terrible!" and covering her face with her hands, she sank back and burst into a convulsive fit of weeping.

"Maude, Maude, what have I said? What can this man be to you, you – ?" then a sudden thought striking her and throwing light on all that had been unexplained, she went on "I fear, Maude, his doom is fixed. The Duke of Gloucester's death alone could save him!"

"But the Duke is himself impeached and is now a prisoner," answered Maude.

"His trial is to take place to-morrow," returned the Queen, "and his acquittal is certain; there is not a shadow of evidence against him. He will celebrate his recovery of power by enforcing the immediate execution of his orders."

"But if the Duke were to die!" exclaimed Maude eagerly.

"Then, Maude, Brother Bernard's life might be saved, I shall then be all powerful and I could save him."

"You can, you will!" was Maude's agonized cry.

"While the Duke of Gloucester lives I cannot, my influence with the King is nothing to his. You Maude could save him, you alone!"

"How, now?"

"Nay, that cannot be so easily answered," returned the Queen.

"Tell me, I implore you, if it is by the sacrifice of my own life. That indeed would be no sacrifice; life is only a burden to me; but if by any means I can save him!"

"Would you save him by a crime, at least what men would call such?"

Margaret hastily withdrew into an inner room, beckoning Maude to follow her. A long, earnest conversation ensued, the exact particulars of which the old chronicler had never heard. Cardinal Beaufort, the queen's confessor,[75] joined them and gave them his counsel and assistance.

---

[75] Cardinal Beaufort was not Margaret of Anjou's confessor.

4

It may be plainly inferred from the foregoing dialogue what had been the true secret of the nun's sorrow and the reason of her forsaking the world.

At the court of Provence, she had met Sir Roger Drury, an English Knight, who was travelling chiefly to consult the learned men of other lands, especially those who were versed in astrology and witchcraft. He mixed little with the gay Provence court, but he had known Sir William Carew in England, and felt it would be uncourteous to refuse to visit him abroad. He came often; for Sir William was a man of some learning and could converse him on the subjects he most loved. Maude always listened with the most intense earnestness to their conversations. The man whom most of her companions looked upon with positive terror possessed for her the most irresistible fascination. He seldom spoke to her, but when he did, his words were gentle and tender yet not condescending. He looked upon her as a child, and he loved and admired her as a charming child, but nothing more. He had adopted even then a somewhat austere and secluded life, and meditated withdrawing to a monastery and there devoting himself entirely to the pursuit of science.

He returned to England before the ambassador and his party. Maude felt that the charm of her life was gone, and feared that her bright dream was over. She never spoke of him, and it was only by accident she learned that he had left the world and retired to a cloister. The place of his retreat, she had never heard, never asked. The blow was borne in silence, but all remarked that she was altered. She tried to forget; she was once on the point of promising her hand to another. But after vain efforts to live as if no shadow had crossed her path, she suddenly took the resolution which doomed her to a life for which she was unfitted, and in which she sought peace in vain. Not until the morning of that eventful 24th February had she known that Brother Bernard and Sir Roger Drury were one and the same. She had seen the face of the dark monk plainly as she passed on her way to the Abbey, and she felt that she could not be mistaken. Margaret alone knew her secret, and through this knowledge tempted her. The idea of dying for the man she loved had often occurred to her; that of committing a crime and incurring danger to save him attracted her. Religion was at a low ebb in those days,[76] and its precepts unhappily had little weight with her. She had a vague longing for death as the only release from pain, but little thought of what might be beyond.

---

[76] Greene evinces a characteristically negative nineteenth-century view of late medieval Catholicism by portraying fifteenth-century Catholics as irreligious and amoral.

5

It was night – the time so sweet to those wearied with labour, so terrible to those haunted by anxiety or remorse. Silence, deep as the grave had fallen on the Priory where all the inmates save one were buried in sleep, each in her solitary cell. In one alone was no thought of rest, but in its stead wild emotions of love and hatred, self-sacrifice and revenge.

Maude was not left to follow the dictates only of her own mad will, but had received minute instructions from Cardinal Beaufort how to perform in silence and secrecy the deed which in her eyes had been exalted from a crime almost into a virtue by the sense of the motive which impelled her to it.

When the hour of perfect stillness in the house had arrived, she noiselessly relighted her extinguished lamp, and softly opened the door of her cell, which, like those of the other nuns, led into a long gallery, at the end of which access was gained into the chapel. As she stole into its sacred precincts, a feeling of awe and terror almost overcame her, but she hurried on. At the back of the altar was a sliding panel which the Cardinal, who knew the place well, had described to her. She soon found it, and when pushed back it discovered a narrow winding stone staircase. Having ascertained that she could open the panel from the inside, and would thus be able to regain the chapel, she slowly and shudderingly descended the steps. They were damp, dark, and covered with green mould, and as she advanced the air became close, almost stifling. On she went through the subterranean passage, her excitement and horror increasing till she came to another flight of stairs, narrower, more steep, and ruinous than the other. To climb them was no easy matter, and the nearer she approached the scene of her intended crime, the more her heart shrunk with horror at the deed. But she was nerved by the thought that she would thus save the life of one whom she absolutely worshipped, and whose life seemed to her worth that of a hundred other men.

The staircase suddenly brought her to a small door which was, she knew, at the back of the tapestry hangings in the room where the Duke was sleeping.

She listened, and heard not a sound but the heavy bell of the Abbey, which told her there was yet *one hour before midnight.*

She opened the door gently, and nothing but the tapestry hung before her. She had in her hand a drug of such deadly power that a few grains scattered on the face would suffice to kill the strongest man.

A moment – and the deed was done, and she stood again in the subterranean passage. The echo of her own footsteps as she went down the stairs sounded dull and hollow. At that moment a violent gust of wind – or was it something stronger than wind? – dashed the lamp from her hand and totally extinguished it. There was scarcely time for her to realize the horror of her position, when she felt a consciousness that a human figure was near her in that terrible place, although she saw nothing. In a moment a powerful grasp was laid on her arm and she felt herself dragged along in the opposite direction to that by which she had come.

Too horrified to speak or to resist, she perceived the ground becoming lower and damper as if water were near. The dripping from the roof and the increasing descent seemed to intimate that they were passing under the bed of a river. The air became still more foul and suffocating. At length, after a gradual ascent, a gleam of light appeared, but it scarcely gave her relief, for she knew not what might be at hand. They reached the light and the air had already become clearer; it came from the chinks of a heavy door which her companion pushed open and they entered a small cell where a light from a furnace was burning. Strange unknown instruments, heavy books and charts, phials of crystal containing curious liquids, and many other signs, showed that it was the retreat of an astrologer or alchemist. A small grated window, high up in the wall, admitted air and light to this gloomy dwelling. Not that Maude had time or sense to observe all this; for a lantern was suddenly held up to her face and she saw by its light a dark tall figure wrapped from head to foot in a black mantle, and in that figure she recognised Father Bernard.

"Is it possible that a woman can have done that terrible deed?" said a deep voice which echoed fearfully through the arched vault.

Maude sank upon the ground and could not answer. He went on in slow and solemn tone, "Tell me at whose instigation you did this awful crime; it is useless to conceal it; the same science which told me that a murder was being committed can tell me all. I have means of knowing even if you refuse to tell." He fixed upon her his dark piercing eyes; she could not withstand the power of his gaze; she felt that she must confess at least a part of her secret. She stammered out the name of Cardinal Beaufort.

"What means did you use?" he asked.

She showed him a few grains of the powder which she still held in her hand. He started and said, "Your doom is sealed – the Cardinal has provided against treachery – your hours are numbered. Do you think poison so strong will not affect you equally with your victim? Its operation will be slower, as you have only held it in your hand, but it is fatal – surely fatal."

Maude started to her feet; a light burnt in her eyes, and her whole form dilated with wild excitement; "I thank the Cardinal," she said, "thank him; for he has spared me the torture and the stake to which your discovery would have brought me. In death I shall find rest."

"Rest!" repeated her companion, "Rest! you know not of what you speak; ages of penance and purgatory must atone for your crime ere rest can come. Your spirit will wander restlessly around the scene of your crime, it may for centuries. You will see those whom you have known and loved pass away and generations follow them. You will see the destruction of this splendid Abbey, of your own Priory, of all that you venerate now. Helplessly you will witness all. And, worse still for you, amid the ruins you will see in after ages a dwelling of comfort and luxury, a home of such happiness as you can never know. You will gaze upon the gay and the young, and in their merry laughter and joyous pastimes you will mix unseen, unknown, shut out from all. Little children's happy voices will sound in your ears, and the talk of the older and wiser telling of love and joy, of stirring interests and active deeds. No one will ever know of your sufferings, your sorrows. Worst of all you will glide with noiseless steps through quiet chambers, where all are hushed in sleep, and bending over their peaceful faces, you will long in vain for repose like theirs."

"Is there no mercy for me, then?" cried Maude again, sinking on the ground, "if you knew my motive surely you would show me some pity."

"What could it have been unless the hope of reward from Queen Margaret?" he returned, in a half pitying, half contemptuous tone.

This idea roused her, and wrung from her all her secret as she fiercely answered, "Reward! what reward could tempt me to a crime? Know, merciless, scornful man, that it was to save your life!"

"Mine? are you mad? unhappy girl," said he starting up in amazement.

"Is not the Duke of Gloucester your enemy? has he not sworn your destruction?"

"He was indeed my enemy," he answered, "I would have met him in fair field in open fight, but would have saved him from midnight assassination, at the risk of my own life. And who are you, and what am I to you that my enemies should be yours?" he went on in a softer tone.

"Has Sir Roger Drury quite forgotten Maude Carew?" she answered proudly.

"Maude Carew!" he repeated, "the fair child of my old friend; I often saw her in Provence; she cannot be a murderer, impossible!"

"It is even so," she said calmly, "to save the life of one more worthy than herself."

"Alas! it is too late to give you aught but pity and the hope of peace after long and dreary wanderings;" he answered gently, kindly, and very sadly.

"My strength is failing, my senses are leaving me, in charity guide me to the Priory again that none may know all that I have done," she said faintly.

He took her hand and supported her half unconscious through the long gloomy passage by which they had come. He found the sliding panel in the Priory chapel and laid her down before the altar. There she was found by the nuns. They deemed she had stolen thither to pay some prescribed office of devotion and there death had overtaken her.

None ever knew the secret of that terrible night. She was laid in the tomb of her family within the precincts of St. Edmund's church.[77] There (let me add to my chronicler's tale) all of that noble family who died before its destruction have been buried, and their descendants now rest in the chancel of St. Mary's church.[78]

Retribution quickly followed the instigators as well as the perpetrator of the crime. Cardinal Beaufort died soon after in great suffering. Queen Margaret was unfortunate and miserable all the rest of her life; her husband was dethroned and murdered; her only son was killed in cold blood after the battle of Tewkesbury; and she herself, fallen from her royal station, spent dreary years as a prisoner in the Tower and afterwards as a dependent on her father's bounty.

At a later time, Brother Bernard had confessed the whole of this dreadful story to the old monk, who chronicled it and concealed the manuscript in his cell. He tells us too that ever since that awful night, the sound of heavy footsteps had been heard by the monks *one hour before midnight*; that

---

[77] A nun would never have been buried in a family tomb, but rather in her monastic cemetery.

[78] The Carews buried in St Mary's church were, in fact, all interred before the dissolution, and there was never a Carew tomb (that we know of) in the abbey church.

many had been conscious of the presence of the phantom nun, though no one knew who or what she was. The sound of her footstep gliding along had often been distinctly heard, and sleepers within the Abbey walls had been roused by the sense that a form was bending over them, whose breathing they could almost hear, and whose shadowy garments could be dimly descried in the darkness. He foretells that, felt and heard but seldom seen, the same phantom shall haunt the precincts of the old monastery for centuries to come, and shall inspire a vague terror into the hearts of many.

There is but one day and one hour in the year when her form will sometimes be perceived. It is on the 24th of February, *one hour before midnight.* She will be seen wandering restlessly through the ruins of the old church where she was buried. Sometimes not one only, but two dark dimly defined forms, will be observed, and around the head of one the faint glitter of a royal crown, showing that Queen Margaret from her distant tomb in Provence joins on that night her companion in guilt, and that the last Queen of the Red Rose line still haunts the scene of her ancient crime.

*

Here the manuscript ends; – we know by experience the truth of the old monk's prophecy; the sound of footsteps is still heard; touches are felt which cannot be accounted for, and those who have courage to search through the ruins on the night of the 24th of February, may yet see perchance the phantom which haunts this ancient and romantic dwelling.

END.

Bibliography

Anolik, R. B., *Property and Power in English Gothic Literature* (Jefferson, NC: MacFarland and Co., 2016)

Cox, J. C., 'Ecclesiastical History' in W. Page (ed.), *The Victoria History of the County of Suffolk: Volume Two* (London: Archibald Constable and Co., 1907), pp. 1–156

Davies, O., *The Haunted: A Social History of Ghosts* (Basingstoke: Palgrave MacMillan, 2007)

Dundes, A., *Folklore Matters* (Knoxville, TN: University of Tennessee Press, 1989)

Frontmatter, *Proceedings of the Suffolk Institute of Archaeology* 1 (1853)

Gottfried, R. S., *Bury St. Edmunds and the Urban Crisis: 1290–1539* (Princeton, NJ: Princeton University Press, 1982)

Greene, J., 'John Lydgate, Monk of Bury', *Proceedings of the Suffolk Institute of Archaeology and History* 10:1 (1898), pp. 7–17

Greene, M., *The Secret Disclosed: A Legend of St. Edmund's Abbey* (Bury St Edmunds: Samuel Gross, 1861)

Harriss, G. L., 'Humphrey [Humfrey or Humphrey of Lancaster], duke of Gloucester [*called* Good Duke Humphrey]', *The Oxford Dictionary of National Biography*, online edition, doi.org/10.1093/ref:odnb/14155

Hartsiotis, K., *Suffolk Folk Tales* (Stroud: The History Press, 2013)

Hills, G. M., 'The Antiquities of Bury St Edmunds', *Journal of the British Archaeological Association* 21:1 (1865), pp. 32–56

Höglund, J., 'Mesmerism and Hypnotism' in K. A. Morrison (ed.), *Companion to Victorian Popular Fiction* (Jefferson, NC: MacFarland and Co., 2018)

MacCulloch, D., *Suffolk and the Tudors: Politics and Religion in an English County 1500–1600* (Oxford: Clarendon Press, 1986)

McAleer, J. P., 'The West Front of the Abbey Church' in A. Gransden (ed.) *Bury St Edmunds: Medieval Art, Architecture, Archaeology and Economy*, British

Archaeological Association Conference Transactions 20 (Leeds: The British Archaeological Association, 1998), pp. 22–33

Milner, J. B., *Six Hospitals and a Chapel: The Story of the Medieval Hospitals of Bury St Edmunds, Suffolk* (Ipswich: Suffolk Institute of Archaeology and History/St Nicholas Hospice, 2013)

Moorman, J. R. H. (ed.), *Medieval Franciscan Houses* (St Bonaventure, NY: St Bonaventure University, 1983)

Murdie, A., *Haunted Bury St Edmunds* (Stroud: Tempus, 2006)

Petrina, A., *Cultural Politics in Fifteenth-Century England: The Case of Humphrey, Duke of Gloucester* (Leiden: Brill, 2004)

Sandford, F., *A Genealogical History of the Kings of England* (London, 1677), 7 vols

Shakespeare, W., *Complete Works of William Shakespeare* (London: Harper Collins, 1994)

Statham, M., *The Book of Bury St Edmunds*, 2nd edn (Buckingham: Baron Birch, 1996)

Tymms, S., *An Architectural and Historical Account of the Church of St. Mary, Bury St. Edmunds* (Bury St Edmunds: Jackson and Frost, 1854)

Vickers, K. H., *Humphrey, Duke of Gloucester: A Biography* (London: Constable and Co., 1907)

Westwood, J., and Simpson, J., *The Lore of the Land: A Guide to England's Legends, from Spring-Heeled Jack to the Witches of Warboys* (London: Penguin, 2005)

Wilson, R. G., 'Greene family (*per.* 1801–1920)', *The Oxford Dictionary of National Biography*, online edition, doi.org/10.1093/ref:odnb/50414

Yates, R., *An Illustration of the Monastic Antiquities of the Town and Abbey of St Edmund's Bury* (London: J. B. Nichols & Son, 1843)

Young, F., *English Catholics and the Supernatural, 1553–1829* (Ashgate: Farnham, 2013)

Young, F., *The Abbey of Bury St Edmunds: History, Legacy and Discovery* (Norwich: Lasse Press, 2016)

Newspaper

'Death and Funeral of Miss Greene', newspaper cutting pasted into Cambridge University Library's copy of Greene's *The Secret Disclosed* (classmark 1861.8.108)

Unpublished report

Hoggett, R., *The Abbey of St Edmund: Heritage Assessment*, unpublished report for the Abbey of St Edmund Heritage Partnership, June 2018

Websites

ancestry.co.uk

Index

ALSO PUBLISHED BY ST JURMIN PRESS

M. H. James, ***Bogie Tales of East Anglia***

Originally published in 1891, *Bogie Tales of East Anglia* by Margaret Helen James was the first book devoted to the folklore of East Anglia. However, the book vanished into obscurity soon after publication, and has never been reprinted until now. Featuring witchcraft, ghosts, charms, traditional cures, legendary tales and an assortment of terrifying spectres (including East Anglia's demon dog, Black Shuck), Margaret James's book is an important source for the folklore current in the Waveney Valley and Suffolk coast in the late 19th century. This critical edition, with an introduction and detailed notes by the folklorist Francis Young, makes available for the first time a rare and elusive book on the supernatural folklore of Norfolk and Suffolk.

ISBN 9780992640460
126pp.
Available from lulu.com

Printed in Great Britain
by Amazon

18835042R00051